NOV -- 2023

WITHDRAWN

WINNETKA-NORTHFIELD
PUBLIC LIBRARY DISTRICT
WINNETKA, IL 60093
847-446-7220

My Food

Published in 2024 by Windmill Books,
an Imprint of Rosen Publishing
2544 Clinton St.
Buffalo, NY 14224

Copyright © 2021 by Miles Kelly Publishing

All rights reserved. No part of this book may be reproduced in any form
without permission in writing from the publisher, except by a reviewer.

Publishing Director Belinda Gallagher
Creative Director Jo Cowan
Senior Editor Becky Miles
Designer Venita Kidwai
Production Jenny Brunwin
Image Manager Liberty Newton
Reprographics Stephan Davis
Assets Lorraine King

Cataloging-in-Publication Data

Names: Lewis, Liza, illustrator.
Title: My food / illustrated by Liza Lewis.
Description: New York : Windmill Books, 2024. | Series: Wonderful words
Identifiers: ISBN 9781538394571 (pbk.) | ISBN 9781538394588 (library bound) | ISBN 9781538394595 (ebook)
Subjects: LCSH: Food--Pictorial works--Juvenile literature. | Vocabulary--Pictorial works--Juvenile literature.
Classification: LCC TX355.L495 2024 | DDC 641.3--dc23

Printed in the United States of America

CPSIA Compliance Information: Batch CSWM24
For Further Information contact Rosen Publishing at 1-800-237-9932

Find us on

WONDERFUL WORDS

My Food

Illustrated by Liza Lewis

WINDMILL BOOKS

Start the day

There are lots of yummy foods we can eat for breakfast. Some are hot and some are cold.

CAN YOU FIND THE LITTLE COW?

strawberry yogurt

waffles

oatmeal

boiled egg

glass of milk

cereal

blueberry jam

What do you like to eat for breakfast? Do you prefer fruit or something cooked?

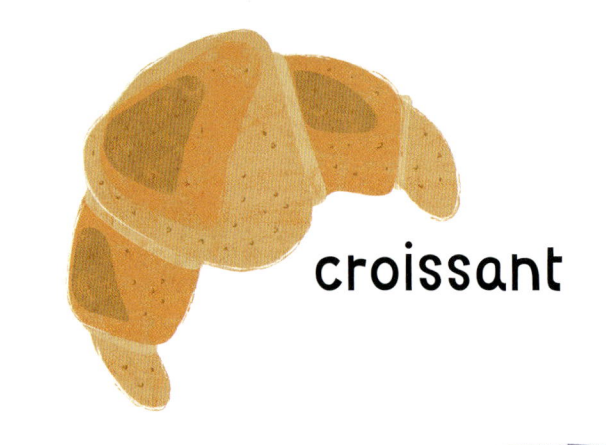

croissant

hot chocolate

fried eggs

bacon

fruit salad

juice

CAN YOU SPOT THE BLUE SAUCER?

toast

HOW MANY EGGS CAN YOU COUNT?

toast and jam

Fantastic fruit

Fruit grows on trees and other plants. It tastes delicious and is good for you too!

HOW MANY CHERRIES CAN YOU SEE?

blackberries

raspberries

orange

watermelon

kiwi

cherries

lemon

pineapple

apple

peach

strawberries

9

We can buy fruit from a market stall or supermarket, or sometimes we grow our own.

blueberries

pear

grapes

pomegranate

market stall

bananas

HOW MANY BLUEBERRIES CAN YOU COUNT?

Going on a picnic

It's lots of fun to have a picnic outdoors. Can you name all of the things you can see?

baguette

HOW MANY SANDWICHES ARE ON THE PLATE?

picnic basket

banana

potato salad

CAN YOU FIND THREE STRAWBERRIES?

cheese sandwich

picnic

sandwich

cookies

cake

apples

bunch of grapes

If you were going on a picnic, what would you like to take?

quiche

CAN YOU COUNT THE SLICES OF TOMATO?

salad

chicken drumstick

pork pie

cucumber

peanut butter and jelly sandwich

green olives

ham sandwich

chips

Grow your own

Some people grow fruits and vegetables in their garden.

beet

carrots

HOW MANY CARROTS ARE IN THE GROUND?

CAN YOU SPOT THE WHITE BUTTERFLY?

peas

vegetable patch

eggplant

Fruits and vegetables are parts of plants that we can eat.

pumpkin

broccoli

potatoes

tomato

zucchini

lettuce

CAN YOU COUNT THE TOMATO SEEDS?

peppers

mushrooms

cauliflower

spring onions

19

Cooking and baking

You can make a delicious cake with flour, eggs, butter, and sugar.

CAN YOU FIND FOUR BROWN EGGS?

bowl and whisk

chocolate cake

flour

WHAT COLOR IS THE MIXING BOWL?

honey

eggs

butter

sugar

Cooking is a lot of fun. You can use all kinds of ingredients.

onion

chives

basil

herbs

chili pepper

pasta

canned tomatoes

WHICH LIDS ARE CLOSED AND WHICH LID IS OPEN?

salt and pepper

spatula

pancake

frying pan

olive oil

rice

garlic

23

At school

Some children bring in a packed lunch while others have a meal from the cafeteria.

banana

ice cream

apple pie

sandwich

milk

apple

packed lunch

24

school lunch

CAN YOU FIND THE GREEN APPLE?

burger

yogurt

fries

salad

glass of water

School lunches can be hot or cold. Which do you prefer?

chicken wrap

ham sandwich

WHERE IS THE SOUP SPOON?

spaghetti and meatballs

baked potato

grated cheese

bread roll

tomato soup

panini

At the fair

Step right up! Come and enjoy some treats at the fair!

candy

popcorn

crêpe

candy stall

lollipop

slushy

CAN YOU SPOT THE PINK BOW?

doughnut

29

Some treats are sweet and some treats are savory. Which are your favorites?

nachos

cotton candy

CAN YOU SPOT THE YELLOW BALLOON?

toffee apple

fries

hot dog

WHAT COLOR IS THE COTTON CANDY?

popsicle

ice cream cone

31

At the bakery

Bread, cakes, cookies, and buns are some of the things you can buy at the bakery.

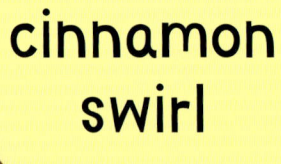

cinnamon swirl

chocolate éclair

baguette

sticky buns

cookie

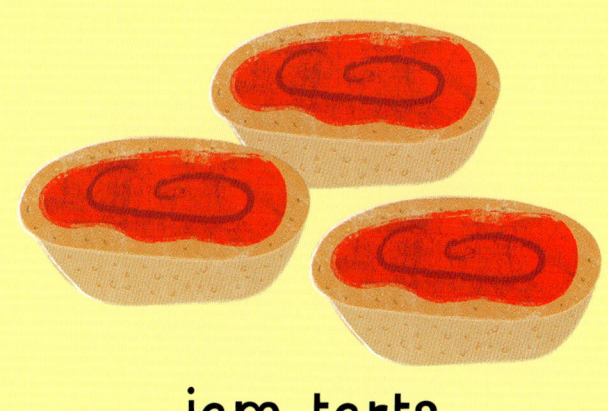

jam tarts

HOW MANY CANDIES ARE ON THE COOKIE?

chocolate pastry

Bakers get up early in the morning to bake the bread each day.

pretzel

loaf of bread

blueberry muffin

CAN YOU COUNT THE SLICES OF BREAD?

baguette

HOW MANY BLUEBERRIES CAN YOU COUNT ON THE MUFFIN?

chocolate brownie

cherry

icing

gingerbread man

sticky bun

35

Barbecue time

In the summertime, it's fun to cook outside on a barbecue.

WHAT COLOR IS THE KETCHUP BOTTLE?

tomato ketchup

barbecue

burger buns

cheeseburger

HOW MANY BURGERS ARE ON THE BARBECUE?

barbecue sauce

corn on the cob

spare ribs

37

At a barbecue, meat, fish and other things are cooked on a rack over hot coals.

CAN YOU COUNT THE LEMON SLICES ON THE FISH?

steak

chicken kebab

fish

lemon slices

potato salad

shrimp

sausage

39

Birthday party!

Are you ready to blow out the candles on this delicious birthday cake?

pizza

cookies

birthday cake

cheese sandwich

HOW MANY CANDLES ARE ON THE CAKE?

strawberries

lemonade

At a party we enjoy fun and games and lots of tasty treats to eat.

cherry tomatoes

cupcake

macarons

pea pods

chips

celery

cucumber

chocolate sauce

wafer

marshmallows

carrot sticks

radishes

ice cream sundae

chocolate milkshake

HOW MANY MARSHMALLOWS ARE ON THE MILKSHAKE?

vegetables and dip

Jell-O

At the supermarket

You can fill a cart with all the food you need at a supermarket.

CAN YOU SPOT THE LITTLE FISH?

apple juice

chocolate

cheese

frozen peas

HOW MANY CANS OF TOMATOES CAN YOU SEE?

tuna fish

cart

basket

rice

noodles

olives

45

Numbers

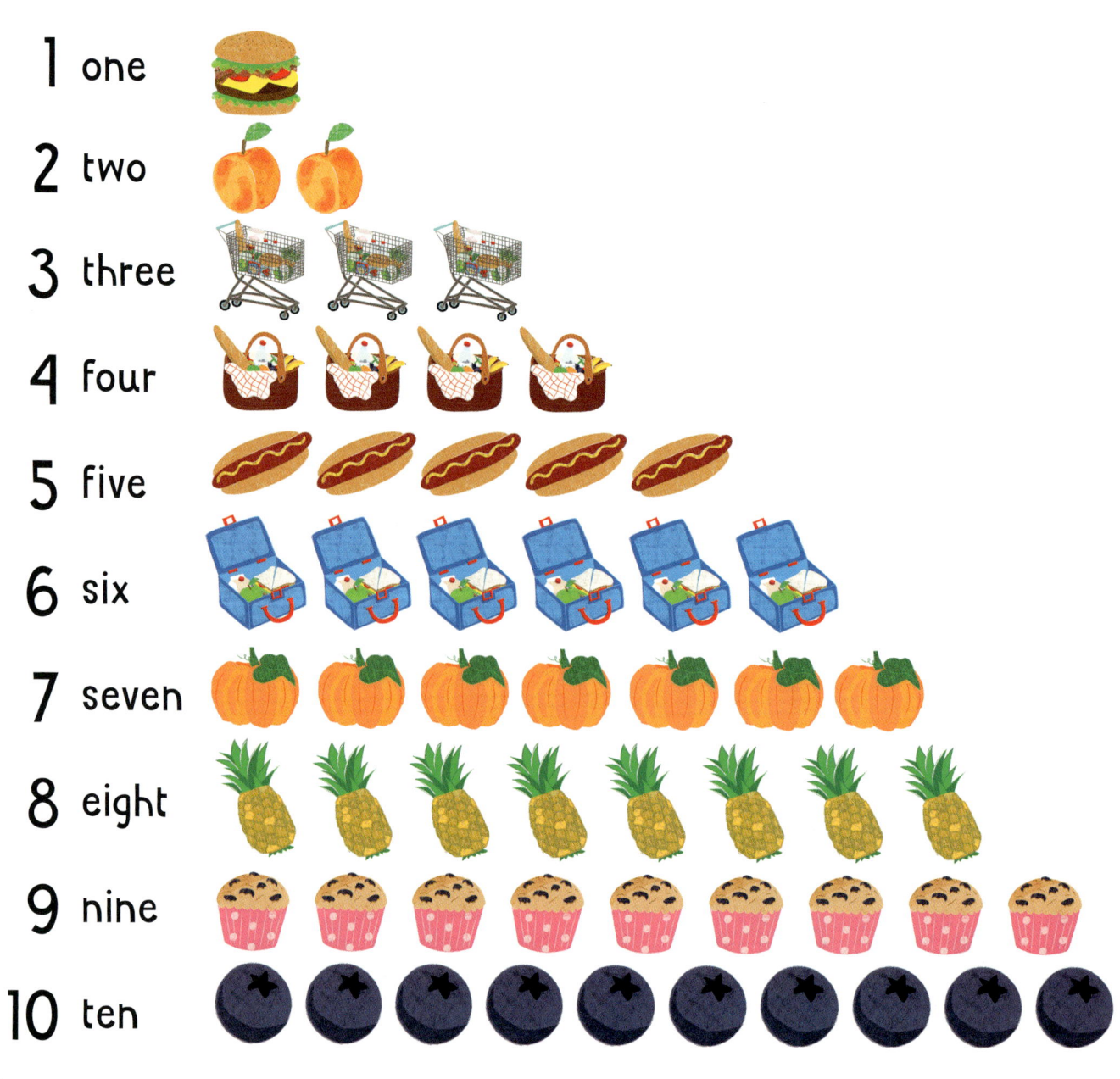

1 one

2 two

3 three

4 four

5 five

6 six

7 seven

8 eight

9 nine

10 ten

11 eleven

12 twelve

13 thirteen

14 fourteen

15 fifteen

16 sixteen

17 seventeen

18 eighteen

19 nineteen

20 twenty

Colors

red
strawberry

orange
carrots

green
apple

brown
onion

white
egg

pink
doughnut

blue
slushy

purple
beet

yellow
banana

silver
fish

48